THE
GODDAUGHTER
Caper

D0972553

ALSO IN THE GODDAUGHTER SERIES:

THE
GODDAUGHTER
Caper

MELODIE CAMPBELL

RAVEN BOOKS
an imprint of
ORCA BOOK PUBLISHERS

Copyright © 2016 Melodie Campbell

All rights reserved. No part of this publication may be
reproduced or transmitted in any form or by any means,
electronic or mechanical, including photocopying, recording or
by any information storage and retrieval system now known or to
be invented, without permission in writing from the publisher.

Library and Archives Canada Cataloguing in Publication

Campbell, Melodie, 1955–, author
The goddaughter caper / Melodie Campbell.
(Rapid Reads)

Issued also in print and electronic formats.
ISBN 978-1-4598-1053-2 (pbk.).—ISBN 978-1-4598-1054-9 (pdf).—
ISBN 978-1-4598-1055-6 (epub)

I. Title. II. Series: Rapid reads
PS8605.A54745G6324 2016   C813'.6   C2015-904468-5
C2015-904469-3

First published in the United States, 2016
Library of Congress Control Number: 2015944546

Summary: In this work of crime fiction, Gina Gallo, mob
goddaughter and unwilling sleuth, gets drawn into a body
caper mystery against her better judgment.(RL 2.5)

Orca Book Publishers is dedicated to preserving the environment and has
printed this book on Forest Stewardship Council® certified paper.

Orca Book Publishers gratefully acknowledges the support for
its publishing programs provided by the following agencies:
the Government of Canada through the Canada Book Fund and the
Canada Council for the Arts, and the Province of British Columbia
through the BC Arts Council and the Book Publishing Tax Credit.

Cover design by Jenn Playford
Cover photography by iStock.com

ORCA BOOK PUBLISHERS
www.orcabook.com

Printed and bound in Canada.

19 18 17 16 • 4 3 2 1

For Cheryl, with Nico's approval.

ONE

"Gina, you have to have red flowers. Whoever heard of a Christmas wedding without red flowers?" Nico waved a hand dramatically through the air.

"Sweetie, I'd rather have pink. You can find pink poinsettias, right?"

He sat back, and his brown eyes went wide. "Pink! My favorite! And black. It's perfect. I can see it now—black tablecloths with ice-sculpture centerpieces. Pink poinsettias on those narrow platforms with streamers coming down from the ceiling..."

1

He was out for the count. I could sip my coffee in peace now. Not that there wasn't peace in this restaurant. It was Monday night, and the place wasn't full.

Nico is my younger cousin, an interior designer, newly minted. He is tall and thin, with bleached blond hair. Nico is starting up an interior-design business next to my jewelry store in Hess Village. He does event planning on the side and is rather enthusiastic about my upcoming wedding. Some might say over-the-top.

Nico isn't gay—he just likes the color pink. So I knew I could get him off the red Christmas kick with a little subterfuge.

We were seated at La Paloma, my uncle Vito's restaurant in the slick part of Hamilton. Okay, don't laugh. The Hammer has some nice places in amongst the steel mills. This upscale bistro is across the street from a major urban teaching hospital. So it's popular with doctors. Doesn't hurt that my other uncle, Vince, donated a whole wing to St. Mary's and sits on its board.

Vince is also my godfather. You may have heard of him. He hails from Sicily and has a number of family businesses I try to stay clear of. This is because I am allergic to prison cells. Let me leave it at that.

"What do you think about peacocks?" Nico said.

I nearly fumbled my coffee cup. *"Peacocks?"*

A crash from the kitchen punctuated that word.

Someone screamed.

"Aunt Vera?" Nico was out of his chair, dashing for the kitchen.

I threw down my linen napkin and jogged right behind him.

The kitchen staff stood like stone statues. I had to push my way to the back, where Vito was standing in front of the open door to the alley.

Aunt Vera, Uncle Vito, Nico and I peered down at a body. It didn't move because it had been recently plugged.

"Oh my *god*, Gina, I can't look. There's blood." Nico hid his face dramatically behind his bent elbow.

"Gina, do you know dis guy?" Aunt Vera poked at him with a wooden spoon.

"Who is it?" Nico said, peeking around his arm.

"Oh jeez. It's Wally the Wanker." Yeah, I knew him. Complete loser from high school. Pilfered the student lockers for cash and blackmail material. Even bigger creep in adult life. Not that Wally was ever an adult, except when it came to buying porn. Hence the nickname.

"Who took him out?" Vera said, rifling through the poor guy's pockets for a wallet. She wasn't as squeamish as Nico.

"Gina, you come with me. I need a calming influence."

4

I followed Uncle Vito's stout body back into the restaurant.

"Everything is *buono, buono,*" he assured the diners. "We just dropped a pan back there."

I walked to my seat, smiling all the way. Big fake smile pasted on my face. Several diners beamed back at me, including a few clients. I nodded to Dr. Drake, who was just sitting down, and to his wife, who had been waiting for him. She grinned widely and flashed her right hand. Big hulking sapphire, recently purchased. I nodded in fake appreciation. No, that's not right. I appreciated her business—truly. I just couldn't think beyond the body at the back door.

I reached my chair, sat down and stared into my cold coffee. Who the hell had shot Wally the Wanker? And why leave him on Vito's doorstep?

Don't get involved, my fickle conscience warned me. *Your wedding is just six weeks away. Your fiancé, is a great guy who has no idea how involved you still are with "the family." Keep it cool, Gina Gallo.*

I should have been calling the cops. But the cops don't like me much, especially Rick Spenser, AKA Spense, another high school non-friend. I didn't think he'd appreciate a call from me. He might even get the impression I'd had something to do with the hit. So I decided not to interrupt his Monday-night poker game.

Maybe ten minutes passed before Nico came out from the back room. He sat down at our little table.

"All taken care of," he whispered. "We can leave now."

Phew! The relief. I couldn't wait to get out of there, to put some distance between me and the recently departed.

I picked up my purse and jacket. Nico followed me out of the restaurant and over to my car in the back parking lot.

When we were all buckled in, I said, "Whew. What a night. Shall I drop you off at your place?"

"Uh, no, not yet, Gina. We have something else to do first."

I pulled onto James.

"And you have to promise not to yell."

I gritted my teeth. "What did you do, Nico?"

"We put the body in your trunk."

"WHAT?" I slammed on the brakes and pulled over. A guy in a big SUV honked his horn twice. He gave me the finger as he passed.

"It was Aunt Vera's idea. She made me help. But don't worry. We've already notified Uncle Vince. We're to take your car to the chop shop. The guys will get it all clean—they promised."

I slammed my palm on the steering wheel. Then I took three deep breaths.

I didn't need to ask how Nico had got the trunk of the car open without my keys. Mark that down to a misspent youth. Nico had a history of B and Es, with a chaser of car thefts. Luckily, he had never been caught. Yet.

"I wasn't going to get involved. I WASN'T GOING TO GET INVOLVED. And now I have a dead body in the trunk of my car. Nico, I could kill you!"

"Don't be silly. There's no more room in the trunk."

Another car honked at us. I shifted back into Drive.

"I'm supposed to be going straight," I said to Nico. "Pete thinks I'm out of it now!" Pete is a sports reporter and my fiancé. I love him to pieces.

Nico tsk-tsked. "Probably you don't need me for this part. Would you mind letting me off home first? It's on the way."

When we got to his condo, I nearly pushed him out.

TWO

It was almost nine. I drove to the place I was supposed to go. (Don't ask—I can't tell you.) It was a little place behind a little place in a not-so-well-lit area. The guys at the chop shop stared as I emerged from the car. They had the good sense not to catcall.

Tony (my second cousin Tony—meaning I have more than one) nodded at me.

"Gina. How's things?" He was wiping his greasy hands on an even greasier towel.

"Same ole, same ole," I said. Except for the dead body in my trunk. "You?"

"Good. The twins are growing. You should come 'round." Tony looks like a Tony. And his wife, Maria, is equally front-page Italian.

He nodded to the trunk. "The Wanker dude?"

I gestured with both arms. "Not my body. I had nothing to do with it."

"Strange they dumped it there at the restaurant. But no worries. I'll get it to the retirement home."

"The retirement home? Too late for that," I quipped. "You mean the funeral home."

Tony stiffened. He tilted his head. "Sure, whatever."

He looked like he was about to say more, then stopped.

Maybe "retirement home" was new slang for "funeral home"? Like you sort of retired from life there?

"No probs. I'll call you when the car's ready," he said finally.

I wanted to get out of there, but it was really dark. And I had no wheels. And I didn't want to be seen at this place, so that meant no taxi.

I called Pete's cell phone. "Hey, can you come pick me up?"

"Where's your car?" Pete asked.

"What?" Pete's voice always does something to me. I might have been a bit distracted.

"Where is your car?" Pete repeated precisely.

"Oh." I thought fast. "It needed a little work, so I took it in to the mechanic."

"Does this have anything to do with the take-out on James?"

I shrieked a bit. Or, at least, that's what Tony said it sounded like.

"What do you know about a murder on James?" I hissed into the phone.

"I work for a newspaper, remember? I hear everything."

"Well, *un*-hear it. And get the others to un-hear it too." Jeesh. All I needed was reporters following me around, and cops following them.

I gave Pete the address.

"I'm still at work. Pick you up in twenty."

Before I could put my cell back in my purse, it started singing "Shut Up and Drive."

"Wally the Wanker got whacked?" It was Sammy the String Bean, Vince's underboss.

I hesitated. "Looks like two plugs from a .38. You mean you didn't do it?" I wasn't going to say *we*. There is no *we* in my vocabulary when it comes to murder.

"No way, Sugar. This is interesting. Gotta go talk to Vince." He hung up.

Sure, it was. Interesting, that is.

I was still mulling it over when Pete drove up in his hot little convertible. I hopped in and didn't look back.

12

* * *

We had a good night in my condo. Early morning was even better. Pete and I might have come from different ethical backgrounds, but in all else we were delightfully compatible. And I was working on the ethics part.

"So. You got a wedding shower tonight, right?" Pete murmured in my ear. We were playing the part of spoons in a drawer. It was a good resting position, and I needed a rest after all that exercise after sleeping.

I groaned. "Don't remind me. I'd rather go three rounds with a crazed gorilla."

Pete liked the boxing metaphor. I knew he would. He is becoming a regular at my cousin Luca's boxing gym. From family accounts, a hit from Pete is like slamming into a brick wall. He can take it just as good.

None of this surprises me. He is a few inches over six feet and used to be a professional quarterback. Those broad shoulders and big arms are packed with muscle.

Just looking at him now made me feel weak in the knees. Knowing what that body could do to me was out of bounds.

"So you won't be needing me tonight," Pete said. "I'll be at the gym if you do." He kissed my shoulder.

I grumbled and rolled out of his arms. "I hate showers. Especially family showers."

Pete laughed. His dark-blond hair was all tousled. I could see his hazel eyes watching me as I left the bed. He smiled and continued to watch. Pete said I had the body of a mythical goddess. Good thing he liked curves.

"I would much rather be with you tonight. You know that." I headed to the bathroom.

He grunted with satisfaction. "You should try to enjoy your own wedding shower, babe."

"Hell's bells, Pete. Would *you* want to be stuck in a room with all the family aunts?"

My back was to him, but no doubt he shivered. My aunts have a reputation. If you think the men in our family are dangerous...'Nuf said.

I waited until Pete had ambled into the bathroom for a shower. Then I called Paulo, my annoyingly handsome lawyer cousin. He was my go-to guy for gossip. I used a burner phone so the call couldn't be traced to me.

"What was Wally the Wanker into?" I asked.

"Officially—parking lots. He cruised the lots looking for vehicles that should be removed, if you get my drift. Unofficially— meaning without the family blessing— drugs. But the upmarket kind. Wally was making a little extra on the side, peddling OxyContin to the upper classes."

I paused for thought. "So he was operating freelance, so to speak?"

"You got it. Vince wasn't crazy about it but turned a blind eye."

I promised to take Paulo out to lunch the next week, then sat back on the bed to think.

The recently deceased was not big on my hit parade. Back in high school, Wally's trade was blackmail. The creep would break into lockers after school and rifle through them to find secrets. I happened to know that Nico had been one of his victims. Luckily, I didn't know this back then, or Wally's life might have been even shorter.

But that got me thinking. Perhaps he was still working that particular operation. Only with big-time adult secrets now. Secrets worth killing for.

I couldn't help but be curious. Who had whacked him, and why?

Leave it alone, Gina, I told myself. *You have enough to worry about. A wedding in six weeks to a fiancé who thinks you've gone straight.* And I *had* gone straight for a whole week.

It was a start.

I should stay out of this. Banish it from my mind.

I finished dressing and went to find Pete.

THREE

Tiffany had already opened up by the time Pete dropped me off at the store. Tiff is my Goth-inspired shop assistant and cousin. She is also Nico's little sister. The store is Ricci Jewelers. I'm a certified gemologist, and I run it for the family. It is probably the *only* family business that is totally legit. I work hard to keep it that way.

I arrived with two coffees, both no sugar, double cream. Tiff was dealing with a customer, a fellow who looked like a refugee from the heavy-metal era.

When she saw me with the coffees, she looked grateful.

"Zak here is looking at gold chains," she said, gesturing to the guy. Zak had as many piercings as Tiff and outdid her in the tattoo department. They both had jet-black hair, but Zak's was longer by about a foot.

Gold chains would certainly stand out against the faded black band T-shirt and tattoo-green neck.

I plunked one coffee down on the counter.

"Cool," I said. I nodded at Zak. He gave me a big-toothed grin. "I'll be in the back if you need me."

I sauntered to my little office, past the white and greenish-blue walls. Sunlight cascaded through the windows, hitting a shelf of Murano art glass. A beautiful rainbow of colors sparkled on the white wall opposite.

I love this store. Usually jewelry stores are full of formal wood, like old banks.

Mine is a radiant and happy place. Nico helped me decorate it. His taste is flamboyant, but I managed to tame him, and the result was splendid.

I entered the office. Just inside the door to the left was a carved wooden box, about four feet long. The carving was really intricate, the sort of thing you see in antique shops.

"Hey, Tiff, what's this?"

"Paulo had someone deliver it," Tiff yelled from the store front. "They said it was from Seb's studio."

This was interesting. Recently, my great-uncle Seb had died of a coital coronary. He'd left his entire estate to me—with strings attached. I'd had to return an extremely valuable painting to the City Art Gallery. (That painting was real. The one hanging in the gallery was a fake. Seb was a good artist and an even better forger.) I had managed to accomplish the switch a few weeks ago, with the help of Nico and the Last Chance Club. More on them later.

I walked over to my desk and put down the remaining coffee. Then I picked up the phone and dialed Paulo. He answered on the second ring.

"So what's in the box?" I asked.

"Seb was old-school. He didn't believe in banks," said Paulo. "Except to rob them, of course. So he never had a safety deposit box."

Even more interesting…

"You'll find bond certificates and cash in there. Some valuable drawings. Most of your inheritance, in fact. Other than the real estate."

Seb had also left me his art studio on James North. I still needed to decide what to do with that.

"This is a little weird," I said, giving the box a slight kick with my shoe. "What should I do?"

"Go through it. Make a list. Get the stuff to a bank as soon as possible. I suggest you talk to Gaetano Gentile at the Royal Bank on King. He does some investments for the family."

Sort of ironic, having one of the family working for a bank. But, as Pete would say, I was related to half the people in this burg.

"The key is in an envelope on your desk. Put that in a safe place until you can get it all to the bank." Paulo rang off.

I found the envelope. The key was inside. Then I went back over to the box. A small padlock hung from an old brass clasp. The key unlocked the padlock, and I twisted the lock open. Then I took the key and put it immediately in the inside zippered pocket of my purse.

I returned to the box—actually, the proper term for it would probably be chest. It was carved, after all. I leaned forward to open the lid. It was heavier than it looked.

Yup, it was crammed with paper. Several big brown envelopes—holding bond certificates, I guessed. To one side I could see wads of old currency bundled up with rubber bands. Heck, there were even some two-dollar bills! When did they stop making those? Were they even legal still?

But there were several stacks of tens and twenties as well.

My nose caught a whiff of mildew. Somehow, it seemed like too much work to sort through this right away. I'd wait until Pete was free, and we could go through it together. Might even be fun. After all, it wasn't every day that a person inherited two million. Pete was darned lucky to be marrying me. Good thing he had proposed before we knew I was inheriting from Seb. Otherwise people might have thought he was marrying me for my money. And *that* would make me see red. I hate when people think that. Bad enough when they accuse women of being gold diggers. But to have people thinking that about my fiancé? That would be demeaning.

I put the lid back down. Then I walked to my desk and sat down in the fake-leather swivel chair. The coffee was now at perfect drinking temperature. I sat back to enjoy it, and my mind started to wander.

I had planned not to think about the body in the ally. But somehow, Wally the Wanker was haunting my mind. I could think of a hundred reasons why a person or persons unknown would want to take him out. Blackmail is a poor career choice.

Thing is, there were probably *too many* people with motive. Finding the right one would be tough.

My cell phone began to sing, and it was Nico.

"Gina?" His voice squeaked an octave higher than usual. "Can you come over? Like, right now?"

Weird. It sounded like he was panting.

"Sure," I said. I clicked the phone off.

Nico was only next door, in the newly rented space that would soon house his interior-design store. The family had provided money for him to set up. Of course, this would come with strings attached, I had warned him. In fact, we had talked about it just last week.

But I can't wait for you to get your money, Gina. I want to set up now, Nico had said.

Look, you don't know what you might be agreeing to. They put money your way...believe me, they are going to want something for it, I'd said knowingly.

Nico wouldn't have to be beholden to them for long. I intended to pay the family back as soon as I inherited from Great-Uncle Seb. Now I could do that. Nico was more like a brother to me than a cousin. I got a kick out of thinking how I could help him out.

I left my office, waved to Tiff and Zak at the counter and pushed out the front door into blazing sunlight.

It could be cold in The Hammer in early November, although we usually didn't get snow until December. But today, with the brilliant sun, I didn't need a jacket for the short trip next door.

I let myself in.

The shop itself looked like a movie set gone bad. The place wasn't open yet. Nico was just moving stuff in. Boxes stood everywhere, piled upon one another. A few were half open, with packing paper spilling out the top.

Some of the contents were already on display. There was a full-size bronze crane to the left of the door. Piles of fabric samples sat on the white marble counter beyond it. The floor between was covered with discarded brown paper and bubble wrap.

Nico was standing just beyond the counter, wringing his hands. No, really. I've never seen anyone wring their hands outside of a movie before. He reminded me of Uriah Heep. The Dickens character, not the rock band.

Of course, he was dressed like he'd just escaped from a vintage rock band of sorts. The black skinny pants and lime-green satin shirt were not standard Hamilton issue. Nico carries a man bag rather than a lunchbox.

"Oh thank *god* you're here, Gina. I didn't know what to do."

He seemed glued to the spot, looking down.

"So what gives?" I wound my way through the boxes.

His eyes darted over to me. They were *huge*. A hand went to his mouth.

"Look here." He pointed down with his other hand. I followed it with my eyes, to the crate on the floor.

It was a wooden crate about six feet long and two feet wide. The lid had been wrestled off. What lay there wouldn't exactly help decorate the store. Unless Nico was planning to cater to vampires.

"Holy hell!" I sucked in air. "A body? Another one?"

The hand that had covered Nico's mouth was now doing double time gesturing in the air.

"I thought it was a statue I ordered from Naples." His voice was a whisper.

I looked down into the box.

"This ain't no Venus de Milo, Nico." No artist in his right mind would bother to sculpt this ugly dude.

"I think I'm going to faint," he said. I watched him sink down on another box and groan. He leaned forward with his elbows on his knees. Both hands supported his head.

Crap. Another body. What was it with bodies these days?

"Do we know this one?" I moved closer to peer at the contents of the crate.

This guy was definitely dead, poor fellow. He looked middle-aged and white, with thinning black and gray hair. Someone had folded his hands over his chest. They looked stark against the black of his suit. I noticed there were rings on both hands. Four of them. Rings, that is, and one had a pretty large diamond in it.

So not a poor man. In fact, he looked like someone important.

"You ever see him before?"

Nico shook his head. "You?"

I considered. "Nope. I seriously doubt if he is from around here."

"How can you tell?" Nico asked.

"Not sure. But he looks foreign, and we don't know him. Where do you think this was shipped from? Is there a label?"

"Couldn't see one."

"Who delivered it?"

Nico shrugged his thin shoulders. "It was Fed-Exed. Several things came at once."

"His suit, then? It looks expensive. Maybe it's Italian? There should be a label somewhere."

Nico glanced over to the crate. "No way am I moving that thing to check." He shivered.

Then his nose twitched. "Funny. He doesn't smell much. I thought dead bodies were supposed to be smelly. Not to mention he's been traveling for a while."

"That's because he's been embalmed, Nico."

"What? Are you serious?"

I shook my head. "Look at the color of his skin. Almost natural. Doesn't look gray at all. Remember Great-Uncle Seb?"

Nico and I had recently visited Seb in the hospital. Unfortunately, he hadn't been in a state to wake up when we poked him to say hello.

Nico groaned. "Yeah, Seb looked dead."

I lowered a finger to test the poor dude's hand. Yup. Definitely dead.

"Strange, huh? Who goes to the trouble of embalming someone and then ships them out of the country?"

Nico groaned again. "This is just too weird."

"Maybe…" I was getting an idea. "Maybe they embalmed him just so he *wouldn't* smell bad and attract attention."

That made sense.

"Why ship him here at all?" Nico wailed. "Gina, what are we going to *do*?"

"Let me think," I muttered. We had to get rid of the body as soon as possible, no question. I didn't have a good reputation with the police. And with Nico—and me— showing up at the dump site of Wally the Wanker…well, you get the picture. Two bodies in one week was over the limit, even in The Hammer.

We had to get rid of it. But how? Where would we take it?

Nico has a talent for reading my mind. "We can't exactly dump it in the bay."

Burlington Bay is infamous for serving as an underwater cemetery. Many of the dearly departed who rest there had been fitted with concrete shoes.

"Nico, we won't even be able to budge this crate, let alone carry it. Not with just the two of us."

There was only one thing to do. I phoned Sammy.

FOUR

Sammy is a wiry guy about fifty with Woody Allen hair. He's also sharp as a shark's tooth. He is my godfather's Jewish cousin and a sort of favorite uncle to me. Yes, we can buy both our matzo and mortadella wholesale in this family.

I adore him.

"Doll, I can't talk now," he said. I could hear a lot of commotion in the background. Outdoor noises, and a lot of *clunks*. Men yelling back and forth in Italian.

"Hold ON!" I yelled into the phone. "There's a dead body in a crate here!"

Sammy cursed. "Damn that Mario. He screwed up again. Call Jimmy. He'll take care of it. Gotta go, sweetheart. Sorry."

I stared at the phone as he clicked off.

"Bloody hell," I said to Nico. "I *knew* it. Sammy knows something about this. Told me to call Jimmy."

"Jimmy?" Nico's voice went up in pitch. "As in *Last Chance Club—speed dating for geezers* Jimmy? Why?"

We stared at each other. This was weird. Jimmy is a very old guy who spent the first part of his retirement in the slammer. The family had a combined release-day-and-eightieth-birthday party for him a few years ago.

A few weeks ago, Jimmy and the Last Chance Club from the Holy Cannoli Retirement Home helped me out on a minor job. Okay, a major heist at the art gallery. Actually, a reverse theft. And if that sounds confusing, you should have seen the actual operation.

"What's Jimmy's phone number?" I asked Nico.

He looked down at his smartphone and did a few finger movements. Then he shot a bunch of numbers at me. I punched them into my smartphone and waited for the pickup.

"Discreet burials," said a shaky tenor voice.

I paused a second.

"*Jimmy?*"

"Shit. Who is this?"

"It's Gina."

I could hear another voice in the background asking who it was.

"Gina," whispered Jimmy to the other person. I heard two voices going back and forth in staccato undertones.

I waited.

"Are you still there?" I said.

"I'm here." Jimmy was back with his ear to the phone.

"What was that about burials?"

"Got confused. Thought I was still talking to Mags. We got a funeral to go to."

Mags was Mad Magda, I knew. Magda is a legend in The Hammer. She helped me with that little art-gallery job a few weeks back. That's when I found out Jimmy and Magda were an item. They had been an item for over fifty years. Someday I needed to talk to her about how to keep the magic going. I was getting married soon, after all.

"Look, I got a problem. Nico was expecting a statue to arrive here."

A pause. "Life-size? Shapely broad in heavy marble?"

I clicked to full alert.

"That sounds like it. He got this other... um, thing instead," I said. I didn't want to say *body*, because I didn't know how secure Jimmy's phone was.

"Wondered what the hell had happened. Hold on a sec, Gina."

He turned away from the phone to talk to someone in person. Magda, I guessed. It sounded like chipmunks chattering back and forth.

Meanwhile, at our end, Nico had progressed to rocking back and forth and moaning.

Now I was starting to get panicky. Jimmy came back on the line.

I said, "Look, can you do something about this? Sammy said to call you. And frankly, we're sort of shook up." No kidding. Wasn't every day you opened a box and found a body.

Jimmy was cool. "Don't worry, Gina. I'll take care of it. You and Nico leave the store for a while. Go get a cannoli or something. Come back after three. Bye."

There was a clue in that sentence. If I'd only caught that "store" clue, it would have saved a lot of trouble.

But I didn't catch it, dammit.

I clicked off and turned my head. Nico was staring at me with the biggest brown eyes you ever saw.

"That was possibly the weirdest phone call ever," I said to him.

FIVE

We got back to Hess Village just after four. Nico dropped me off at Ricci Jewelers and went to park the car. Tiff was saying goodbye to a customer on the phone when I walked in the door.

She put the receiver down and looked over. "All ready for the shower tonight?"

I put on a big fake smile. "Sure. It will be swell."

She smirked. It went with her black spiked hair really well.

I hated the idea of a bridal shower, and Tiff knew it. A whole room of women

41

playing those cute games...it's just not me. But that wasn't the only reason. Any sort of gathering that includes my family seems to go lunatic. I try to avoid family events when I can.

But I wouldn't be able to avoid this one. All the aunts would be there, and half of The Hammer.

I walked back to my office and found the door blocked by a large wooden box. Another box! The Hammer seemed to be littered with them these days.

This one was a light wood like pine, and it had a hinged top. A plain steel padlock secured the lid on one side.

"What the hell is this?" I said. I gently kicked the thing with my foot. The box didn't move.

"I think it's a wedding present," said Tiff.

"Cool!" I might not like wedding showers, but wedding presents were a whole other

42

thing. And this one looked unusual. "How do I get it open?"

"Mario left a key." She came around the side of the counter and handed it to me.

I took the steel key. Then I bent over and held the padlock in my left hand. My right hand worked the key.

Click.

I opened the padlock and removed it. I put it on the counter, with the key still in it so it wouldn't get lost.

"Wow," I said. "This lid is heavy. Give me a hand."

Tiff leaned down, and we both struggled with the wooden lid. It swung back on its hinges.

The inside of the box was stuffed with hundreds of those Styrofoam peanuts.

"This is weird," I said. "What can it be?"

Tiff was already scooping handfuls of peanuts and throwing them on the floor.

I let her continue because she was younger than I was and my back was getting sore.

After a while she stood up. We both gazed down at the contents.

A statue.

"That's strange," said Tiff.

I'd seen a lot of marble statues on my various trips to Italy. This one looked museum quality. Maybe a Roman reproduction? Her hairstyle was certainly Roman.

This had to be Nico's missing statue. The one that should have been delivered to his store instead of the body.

I was getting a really funny feeling now. You know that sensation when everything feels tingly? My mind was equally uneasy.

I continued to stare down at the statue. It was rather beautiful, in a Roman Forum kind of way. Not exactly condo sized. "You said Mario brought this?"

"Yeah. And he took away the other one you wanted removed."

My head shot up. "Huh? What other one?"

She tilted her head and met my eyes. "The other box. The smaller one in your office. He said you knew about it. You called Jimmy or something."

What? They took the box full of Seb's stuff? What the poop was going on?

Wham, wham, wham!

Someone was hammering on the glass front door.

I turned. Nico was standing on the other side of the glass. His arms were flailing, and he was generally freaking out. Tiff moved swiftly to unlock the door and let him in.

He burst into the room, brown eyes blazing.

"It's still there!" he blurted.

"What's still there?" I said.

His face was red, and he was panting hard.

"The body!"

I gasped. "In the crate next door?"

"What body?" said Tiff.

We both stared at her.

"CRAP!" I yelled. My arms also flailed. I started to pace. Correction—I tried to pace. The Styrofoam peanuts made it difficult. My foot slipped on them.

"Sonovabitch!"

"What body are you—"

"Quiet," I ordered Tiff. I reached down to rub my ankle. "I'm trying to think."

Body next door. Statue here. Mario screwing up, Sammy had said. Mario was always screwing up.

Bingo! I had it now. I straightened and fixed my eyes on Nico.

"The first box was delivered by a real delivery company, right? Not our guys?"

Nico nodded.

"Then it's simple. Our guys got the place wrong. I called Jimmy on my cell

46

from here this morning. He probably thought the body had been delivered *here*, instead of next door. So he told Mario to return the statue *here* and pick up a box from *here*, instead of your place."

"Oh fiddle, Gina. That has to be it." Nico groaned.

"Right," I said. "Mario was told to pick up a box. But he took Seb's box instead of the one with the body."

"Wouldn't they have noticed it was a bit small for a body, Gina? I mean, the thing couldn't have been longer than three or four feet."

I cocked my head at him. "This is Mario we're talking about here, Nico."

"Oh right," he said. "Silly me."

Mario was not exactly a rocket scientist. In fact, our younger cousin Mario would have trouble spelling rocket scientist. Even if his life and his black curly hair depended on it. He's particularly proud of that hair.

"*What* box? *What* body? I'm, like, totally confused," said Tiff.

We both looked blankly at her.

"You explain it to her," I said finally. "I'm going to call Jimmy."

I walked over to the front door to get some distance. In the background, I could hear Nico and Tiff talking quietly.

Jimmy didn't pick up. I looked at my watch and figured it was probably dinnertime at the Holy Cannoli Retirement Home. He'd be downstairs, because they never missed a meal. Believe it or not, food at the Holy Cannoli is first-rate. This is because the family owns it. My aunts believe serving lousy food is a mortal sin for which you go to hell. This might be superfluous, as a good many of my family have reservations down under just waiting for them.

Next, I tried calling Sammy. He didn't pick up either. What the hell was going on that he wasn't answering his cell phone? Or rather, what was going down right now, and why didn't I know about it?

I was fuming now. That blasted Mario and his thugs had walked off with my inheritance!

"But what am I going to do about the body next door, Gina?" Nico wailed.

You know that famous painting *The Scream*? Nico looked like *The Scream*. I am extremely fond of Nico and don't like to see him upset. So I came up with a plan immediately.

"I can't reach Sammy on the phone. He's probably at the chicken coop. We'll go to the chicken coop right now and catch him. He'll know what to do."

"Can I come?" said Tiff.

I frowned at her. "No. I need you to stay here in case someone comes back for the body next door."

Her face lit up. "So I get to see the body?"

Tiff is made from entirely different cloth than her brother Nico.

"Yes. You get to *guard* the body. Even better."

"That rocks!" she said. "Can I tell Zak?"

Nico groaned. I pulled him by the arm out the door.

SIX

In case I haven't mentioned it before, we have a chicken coop on the shores of Lake Ontario. It's been in the family since the time people really kept chickens.

It's actually a small cottage that is used by the family for storage. And private meetings, if you get my drift. We still call it the chicken coop because it is registered as that for tax reasons. They don't charge much for chicken coops, even when the chickens have a glorious view of Lake Ontario.

We got to the chicken coop in under ten minutes. I drove—otherwise it would have been twenty.

We took Nico's Volkswagen Beetle because my car was still in the shop. My being carless was going to be a drag if it lasted much longer. I needed to call Tony's garage about that.

On the way there, I stopped for a red light. Nico had been quiet until then.

"What do you think really happened to Wally the Wanker?" he asked.

"I think he was playing his old game of blackmail," I said. The light turned, and I pushed the accelerator. "Thing is, this isn't high school, and the mark wasn't a teenager."

"Who do you think it was?"

"Not sure yet," I said. "But I'm working on it."

Damn right, I was. Poor Wally had made an unscheduled trip in the trunk of my car. That kind of made it my business.

I pulled off North Service Road into a narrow lane. It was deserted, but I've been well trained. The gravel driveway had a tale to tell. Something heavy, like a midsize truck, had been there recently. Lots of men had been moving things. You could tell by the footprints.

The driveway was empty now, except for our car.

"Doesn't look like there's anyone here," said Nico.

"Let's go check, just to make sure. Sometimes Sammy gets dropped off here if he doesn't want to draw attention to the place. Which reminds me. I should maybe park across the road, behind the old Melbourne place. This car is rather conspicuous."

Red. Of course, Nico had to buy a red Beetle. My car, on the contrary, is a nondescript little sedan. I don't like to draw attention to myself, considering the business I'm in. Not to mention the family I belong to.

"Good plan," said Nico.

I parked, and we crossed the street. No traffic coming in either direction.

I strode up the gravel driveway to the front of the cottage, which faced the lake. Nico was right behind me. I worked the numbers on the padlock. Then I removed the lock and swung open the rickety wooden door. We walked in.

Nico reached for the cord that operated the single lightbulb hanging from a wire in the center of the room. It clicked on.

It took a few moments for my eyes to adjust to the dimness.

Last time we'd been to the coop, the place had been filled with cartons of cigarettes. Apparently, they had fallen off the back of a truck. These had been sent on to their final destination. Something else stood in their place now.

I stared in horror.

"*Oh my god*, Gina," Nico squeaked.

I gulped. "Coffins. Why are there so many coffins here?"

Coffins were stacked against the entire east wall of the cottage. There had to be at least a dozen, stacked three high along the wall.

"There's nobody here. At least, nobody still alive," Nico said in a shaky voice. "Let's go."

"Wait a minute," I said. "I'm tired of not knowing what's going on. First, Wally the Wanker is taken out by people unknown, and we find him. Not only that, he gets a ride in the trunk of my car. Then a second body turns up in your store. And now...coffins."

"You think those things are related?" Nico said.

"I don't know. But I'm sure going to find out." I stared at the wall of coffins.

Of course, that wasn't the only thing I had to do today. The list of things was growing longer. I still had to find out where my blasted box of boodle got moved to.

This was nuts. I was the goddaughter of the local crime boss, not friggin' Nancy Drew.

"Wait a minute. Does this seem weird to you? Usually I'm involved—albeit kicking and screaming—in pulling off jobs myself. Not playing the part of detective."

Nico shook his head. "It isn't natural. We should get out of here."

"Don't you at least want to see if these coffins are empty?" I flung my purse on the small wooden table and started over to the stack.

"Gina, I really don't think this is a good idea." Nico edged his way backward toward the door.

"Bring that chair over here. I'm going to peek inside one."

Nico groaned. "This is a terrible idea. I just know it."

"Bring it," I ordered. Nico is younger than me and used to taking my orders. Okay, so I had been a bossy kid when we were young.

He dragged the old wooden chair over to the stack of coffins.

"Hold it steady for me," I said.

He held the top of the chairback on both sides. I reached with my right hand to balance myself and climbed onto it. I straightened. The topmost coffin on this stack of three was within reach.

"Doesn't appear to have a lock. I'll just lift the lid and peek."

I tried. I really tried. But the darn lid was so heavy, I couldn't budge it from one end.

"The leverage is wrong," I said sadly. "One would have to get in front of the thing and lift the lid from the middle to raise it."

Nico breathed out in relief.

"This is really none of our business, Gina. We should get out of here."

"One thing for sure," I said, running my hand along the surface of the closest one. "These coffins aren't very good quality. They look like pine, not oak. And not very good pine. Look at this finish, Nico. Definitely substandard."

This was baffling. Our family used only the best oak for coffins.

"Maybe they're made in China?" Nico said.

Now why did that ring a bell? A very distant bell, but now the word *China* was flashing like a neon sign in my head.

The old-fashioned black phone on the wooden desk trilled.

Nico and I stared at each other. His brown eyes were wide.

"Should we answer?" he asked.

I hesitated, then nodded. "Might be important." I reached for the receiver.

And then I waited, like we had been trained. "Wait for the other guy to identify himself"—rule twenty-seven in the soon-to-be bestseller *Burglary for Dummies*.

"Who is this?" said the smooth voice on the other end. I recognized it.

"Paulo?" I said. It was my hoity-toity lawyer cousin.

"That you, Gina? What are you doing there?"

"Trying to find Sammy."

"Get out right away! The cops are coming to raid the place. I got an inside tip."

"Shit!" I yelled. I could hear sirens in the distance. "Are those sirens at your end?"

Paulo cursed. "No. Get in the cubby." He hung up.

I stared at the receiver. *Cubby*? What was he talking about?

I looked over to find Nico wringing his hands.

59

"Paulo said to get in the cubby," I told him.

Nico's face cleared. He nodded.

That didn't help me. "What is he talking about?"

The sirens were getting louder.

Nico sprinted to the little room at the back of the cottage. I followed. The back wall of the room was paneled in knotty pine. Nico pressed a knot with one hand and pushed with his other. A narrow panel opened inward. Nico squeezed through the opening and then signaled for me to follow. He went to the right. I followed on his tail. Then he signaled for me to close the door and latch it from the inside with the small hook and eye.

We stood in a space maybe two feet deep that ran the length of the room. It was dark but not pitch-black in the cubby. I had no trouble working the hook-and-eye closure. I also had no trouble seeing a huge spiderweb about two inches from my face.

"Eep," I squeaked.

Nico shushed me. I could hardly hear him over the sirens.

I looked up and saw that the wall did not go all the way to the roof. That's how the light was getting in from the other room.

Waiting was hell. I am no good at waiting.

Also, my head itched. I tried not to think of what could be making it itch. Creepy-crawlies? I shivered.

The sirens stopped abruptly. Car doors opened and slammed shut. Men stomped and yelled orders. I heard the wooden door being opened...footsteps on the cottage floor. It creaked from the weight of several bodies.

At least these ones were still alive.

Male voices were muffled by the scraping sound of heavy things being moved.

The coffins! Obviously, the cops were finding out what was in the coffins. I gulped.

Nico and I stayed perfectly still. I glanced at him. His eyes were shut tight.

I tried to count how many coffins were being moved, but it was hard. As one was being opened, another was being taken down from the stack. But they looked into at least six. I counted the number of heavy lids that were let go.

All in all, I expect we weren't in the cubby more than ten minutes. But during that time, I got to thinking. How did Nico know about the cubby, and why didn't I? What had he been doing for Sammy over the years that I didn't know about? And what would have put him on the inside of this little secret?

I didn't know whether to be disgruntled or relieved.

At last the men started to leave. I found myself holding my breath as the wooden door slammed shut for the last time. Then we heard car doors closing and engines starting up. They didn't bother to use sirens on the way out.

I waited until the engines were out of earshot. Then I looked over at Nico. He signaled for me to undo the hook from the eye. I wiggled toward him and pulled the door inward.

"That was close," I said, squeezing out. Nico was right behind me. "Good thing I parked across the street."

"That was smart," said Nico. "God, I hate being confined like that. It was everything I could do not to cry like a baby."

I brushed the cobwebs off my top and pants, carefully looking for unwanted critters that might have been hoping to ride piggyback.

"Not only that, but I have to pee," Nico said.

"That's one thing this cottage doesn't have," I said, walking through the doorway to the main part of the cottage.

I stopped dead.

"It used to have an icky outhouse, but that got torn down years ago," said Nico as he came through the doorway. "What a mess—"

He stopped dead.

A cop was sitting on the little wooden table not five feet from us. One I knew quite well.

Spense. He was holding my purse in his lap.

Crap. My purse. I'd left my bloody purse on the table.

"Well, well. Look who we have here," he said. I will never forget that smile on his face.

"Holy shit, we're screwed," said Nico.

They had left one squad car in the driveway. Spense bundled us into the back of it.

I don't know if you have ever been in the back of a cop car before, but there isn't much room. Nico's knees were practically under his chin. They do that on purpose, of course, so it's hard to escape.

And I surely did want to escape.

Rick Spenser. The *last* guy I wanted to see at a time like this. He'd once called me "the girl with the longest confession." He was referring to church, of course. We go way back.

Back to St. Bonaventure Catholic Secondary School, in fact, where he followed me around like a lovelorn creep, hoping to cop a feel. And now the creep wore a cop uniform. The fact that he still thought I was hot was no secret in this burg.

But I am allergic to cops. And tall, thin Spense never was my type.

"Um...sir?" Nico stammered. "Are we being charged with anything?"

"Shut up," said Spense nicely. "I'm taking you in for questioning."

My mind churned. On the way out of the cottage, we had walked between the coffins that were strewn everywhere. The place was a mess. Some were still open. Each was lined with dove- gray satin.

All were empty.

So what was Spense going to question us about?

SEVEN

I don't like cop shops. Believe it or not, I'd had the grand tour of this one before. Didn't appeal to me. Too much gray in the color scheme, and the company sucked.

Nico was shaking beside me, so I figured he felt the same way. I put my hand on his arm to reassure him and decided we shouldn't hang around for long.

So I didn't use my one call to phone Sammy. I didn't phone Uncle Vince or my lawyer cousin Paulo either.

Nope. I called the one person guaranteed to get me out of this place in the blink of an eye. Or, more correctly, the opening of a mouth.

It worked.

Aunt Miriam arrived at the cop shop with the family SWAT team. Aunt Vera, still in her restaurant apron. Aunt Pinky, in one of her gorgeous designer ensembles. And Aunt Grizelda, carrying her thick leather handbag with the brass corners.

You don't want to get near Aunt Griz with that handbag. Hardened criminals have been known to cower.

Aunt Miriam didn't need all the aunts, of course. It was an unnecessary show of force.

I watched from the wooden chair in the corner as Spense rose to greet the liberation army.

Miriam marched right up to him. She came up to his chin, maybe. She also had a good twenty pounds on him.

It didn't surprise me. But it might have surprised some of the cops in the joint when Spense went white.

"Here's a bill of sale for those coffins. It's all in order. We got a deal from China." Miriam shoved a piece of paper in his face.

China. That word again.

"You gonna charge Gina with sompting?" said Miriam. "'Cause our Gina doesn't do nothing wrong. She's a good girl."

"Unlike some," said Aunt Griz, swinging her weapon ever so slightly.

Miriam stared Spense in the eyes, her face grim. I could see him starting to sweat.

"We got an engagement, see? It's Gina's wedding shower. So we gotta leave right now or we'll miss it. They don't like it when you're late for your own shower." Her voice had that unique lilt that made formerly brave men duck for cover.

"Now Mrs. Goldman, you know I have to do my job here—"

"How is your dear mother?" Miriam interrupted. "I haven't seen her since you left school. You remember St. Bonaventure Secondary School, don't you, Richard? I think it's time I paid her a visit, don't you?"

Silence. A whole lot of silence. There were at least five other cops in the room, plus a few customers. Everyone in the place had stopped to listen.

Spense's Adam's apple bobbed.

The room was thick with tension. I glanced from my aunt to the unfortunate Spense. This could only mean one thing. What the heck did Aunt Miriam have on Spense?

"You can go, Gina," Spense said thickly. "And you too, fancy-pants. But don't leave town."

"I'm getting married in a few weeks. Why would I leave town?" I shrugged and reached for my purse and jacket.

The station was completely silent as the aunts and Nico filed out. I hung back a bit. I turned to Spense, who was watching me with his arms crossed. He wore the frown that he always reserved for me.

"You wouldn't like to lock me up for a bit, would you?" I said to Spense. "Just till the shower is over." I really do hate showers.

"Get outta here, Gina," he said, waving a hand.

I caught up with the others in the parking lot. Miriam was nearly to her car. I put my hand on her arm.

"Thanks a mil for getting us out of there, Auntie M. But what the heck do you have on poor Spense?"

Miriam stopped walking. She smiled. It wasn't nice.

"Remember I was a lunch monitor at St. Bonaventure." It was a statement, not a question.

Uh-oh. This was going to be good. I just knew it. Nico stuck his head forward to hear.

She told us.

Nico gasped. "No!!"

Miriam nodded. Both her chins waggled.

I grinned. Spense the voyeur, sneaking into the girls' change room. No doubt getting an eyeful from a hidden corner. Caught in a particularly disgraceful act by our Auntie M. "No wonder he didn't want his mother to know."

"That boy oughta be blind by now," said Miriam.

Nico guffawed.

Miriam marched off, holding her head high.

EIGHT

The event: THE SHOWER

The location: Aunt Pinky's modest mansion near the top of the Niagara Escarpment. Okay, not so modest. Nobody really needs an indoor *and* outdoor pool.

The cast: Aunt Miriam, Aunt Pinky, Aunt Griz. Maria, Tiff, my second cousin Del, who is a few years older than me. I like her a lot. Several more female cousins of aunts, friends of aunts, and cousins of cousins. (No men, of course. Not even Nico. All the men in Pinky's family had vamoosed to the family pool hall.) The mayor's wife.

The wives of several important businessmen from The Hammer. All wearing the latest designer clothes. All sporting expensive rings and jewelry that had been purchased from my store.

We were seated in Aunt Pinky's stunning "great room." The windows overlooking the valley were at least two stories high. In summer, when everything was in bloom, the view took your breath away. It was dark out now, so there wasn't a lot to see except a few lights twinkling in the distance.

When the furniture was pushed to the walls, the room could handle over a hundred guests for cocktails. Today, it held a modest thirty or so, with ample space.

I looked around at the smiling, chatting faces and felt my heart swell. Almost every female I knew and loved was in that room.

Missing: my mom and future mother-in-law, who were still in Florida. They'd be here for the wedding. And Lainy couldn't be here because she was on tour in the deep south.

Everyone has heard of my oldest and dearest friend, of course. She's the Lainy in Lainy McSwain and the Lonesome Doves, the biggest new country singer to come out of Canada since Shania Twain.

Lainy would be my maid of honor on "the day."

Tiff sat beside me on the caramel suede sofa. She was wearing black on black, as usual. Pinky sat on the other side. She lived up to her name. That was one gorgeous hot-pink dress.

Pinky handed me the first gift box. It was from Lainy. I read the card out loud.

"Sorry to miss yer party, hon. I'm in Louisiana tonight, and the 'gaters are rising. But wanted to send this little gift and a big fat hug. See y'all at the rehearsal dins, where I'll be singin' a new song for you and the stallion.

Oh, and tell Nico that Pauly has found a girl-friend. Hugs and kisses."

Lainy called Pete "the stallion." He seemed to like it.

And Nico would be glad to know that Pauly the parrot had a new interest. His previous interests were swearing and pecking. That got old pretty quick.

And so the fun began. I tore into the wrapping paper like a six-year-old kid.

To be clear on showers—I don't mind the opening-gifts part. The opening-gifts part was cool. I got a lot of kitchen stuff and some pretty lingerie. The lingerie was, of course, from Lainy. Pure-silk black satin, and not a lot of it. Pete would like it. Of course, Pete wouldn't care if I wore a burlap sack, whatever the heck that was.

Also regarding showers—I don't mind the food part. To quote Lainy, I am "right partial" to finger sandwiches and Italian pastries.

And the highly potent alcoholic punch was just fine. I had already chugged the first glass they gave me. I was working on the refill now.

What I hated was the silly paper-plate hat Pinky insisted on making for me. What long-ago sadist decided that gift bows should be made into a freaking hat? Every woman in this room could have afforded the plane fare to Paris, France, just to pick out a new chapeau. Yet here they were, making me wear a bunch of dollar-store bows on my head. Assorted ribbons hung down from the brim. They tickled my nose.

"Let's take a photo," said Del with a twinkle in her eye. She held up her smart-phone.

"Let's remember I know your secrets," I said to her in return. "And all the aunts are in this room."

"Oh right." She put her phone back in her purse.

I wore the hat for a few minutes to keep Pinky happy. It fell off three times and finally stayed off.

"Your hair is all staticky now!" Tiff giggled.

I tried to smooth it down with my hand and muttered, "I need some more punch."

"Don't forget you have a hair appointment tomorrow afternoon, Gina." Mandy waggled a finger at me. She was a cousin of a cousin and ran a high-end salon in town.

"Sure. Looking forward to it." That was a lie. I hated getting my hair done almost as much as I hated wedding showers.

Del handed me a new glass of punch. I smiled my thanks and got to it.

"Forgot to tell you," Tiff said. "Mrs. Drake came into the store today after you left. She wants to have earrings made to match the sapphire ring."

I whistled low. "That will cost a bundle. Double of everything." Earrings come in twos.

"Who is Mrs. Drake?" asked Del.

"A customer of mine at the store," I said. "Her husband is a well-known doctor in town."

"Are you talking about Sherry Drake?" Pinky piped up. "They just bought a condo in Scottsdale, Arizona."

I turned my head. "I didn't know you knew her."

Pinky's smile could melt the coldest heart. "Sure I do. My husband is a doctor, remember?"

And so was Sherry Drake's husband. Sometimes I could be a ditz.

"I heard there were a lot of bargains in Arizona after the recession," said Aunt Griz. "Places were going real cheap."

"This one wouldn't have been cheap," Pinky said. "It's the new condo right next to Nordstrom at the Scottsdale Fashion Center."

I watched several women nod. Then the conversation morphed into the merits of Nordstrom versus Neiman Marcus.

"Sucks that everyone but us knows exactly where that place is," grumbled Tiff.

I had been thinking the same thing. Last spring, I went to Arizona with Pete for exactly one day. There wasn't a lot of time to look around, because we were kind of busy. Pete likes to call that episode "The Great Shoe Fiasco." I prefer to think of it as "Gina Bails Out the Family Yet Again." But Pete and I got together on that trip, so I'm not complaining.

I had a cool idea.

"Tell you what. Why don't I fly us down there for a few days after I get my inheritance finalized?"

Tiff's brown eyes popped. "Really? You mean it?"

"Sure." I smiled. "Just us girls. I know they have an international gem show down there in February. It's supposed to be fab. We should go."

"Gina, you're the best."

I couldn't believe how happy it made me to see Tiff excited. Having a little extra money was going to be grand.

"So what's our timeline with the earrings?" I asked.

"She didn't say. Mrs. Drake wants to talk to you personally. The weirdest thing, though"—Tiff leaned toward me and lowered her voice—"she wants to pay in cash."

My eyebrows went up. "That's unusual."

"Maybe she doesn't want a paper trail? So her husband doesn't know how much she's spending?"

"Could be," I said slowly. "Or maybe her husband isn't footing the bill."

Tiff's wide brown eyes got bigger. "You mean she's having an affair?"

I shrugged. "Ours is not to reason why."
Or, at least, not to spill the beans. As long
as the cash wasn't counterfeit, I didn't care
where it came from.

Counterfeit! I snapped my fingers. That
was it! That was the China connection.

Counterfeit, Chinese, coffins...

I must have hollered out loud, because
several heads turned to me.

"I was just remembering something I
had to do," I said to explain. Gad, my voice
sounded loud.

That's when they started the stupid
party games. I slugged back the rest of the
punch in my glass. Someone handed me a
piece of paper.

"What the hell is this supposed to be?"
I whispered to Tiff and pointed.

IMDBDRIESA

My eyesight was going wonky.

"It's a real word," she said. "You have to
unscramble it."

Did I mention that I hate stupid shower games?

"Gina! Are you girls cheating?" It was Aunt Miriam's voice. I instinctively trembled and prepared for another hour of misery.

"Punch!" I yelled in desperation. Del appeared with a new glass, and I drank it down in one go.

NINE

The next morning I was still without a car. Pete picked me up at my condo. I didn't even have to ask him to come and do it. That's the kind of guy he is.

He dropped me off at Ricci Jewelers and continued on to the *Steeltown Star* newspaper office.

The first thing I did was phone Jimmy at the retirement home. He answered on the first ring.

"Hi, Gina."

"Where's my box?" I blurted into the phone. Getting Seb's box back was my absolute first priority.

Pause. Sounds of confused chatter. Mad Magda must have been in the room.

I sighed. "The one that came from my store. Mario and gang picked it up by mistake yesterday."

"Oh. That box. I think we buried it."

"WHAT?"

"Last night."

"You *buried* it?"

"It was a nice service. You would have liked it."

My box got a funeral?

"It wasn't supposed to be buried, Jimmy! They took the wrong box."

More commotion. Mad Magda came on the line.

"Gina, don't panic. We can unbury it. I know exactly where it is. Meet us at Black

Chapel Cemetery at eight tonight. Bring a few strong lads with shovels."

She rang off.

I stared at the phone in my hand. My inheritance got its own funeral. This family was freaking nuts.

What the poop was going on? I had to talk to Sammy about this. Meanwhile, I tried to look on the positive side. Something had been accomplished. At least I knew where Seb's box was, and that it was safe. What a relief! Nico and Pete could help me get it back that night.

My head was pounding. No more bridal-shower punch for me—not ever. I was having trouble thinking straight.

I handled the store customers for a while as best I could. Tiff came to relieve me at noon.

"Do you have any aspirin?" My voice was unusually high and shrill.

She grinned and handed me the takeout coffee she had brought for me. Then she reached into her shoulder bag.

Aspirin with a chaser of coffee. My favorite lunch.

"Don't forget that hair appointment," she said.

"Rats. I don't have a car." Maybe I could get out of it.

"Nico will lend you his. He's next door. Ask him."

Drat Tiff. She always had an answer for everything.

And so Nico lent me his little red Beetle for the day.

"This is really nice of you," I said to him.

He threw me the keys.

"Don't be silly, Gina. I don't need it. I'll be here all day sorting through stuff. Besides, think of all the things you do for me."

That was generous of him. Because really what I do most is get him into trouble.

I blew him a kiss and took off to run a few errands. Then I prepared to meet my fate at the hair salon.

Hair Today Gone Tomorrow is more upmarket than the name would lead you to believe. We have a thing about cutesy names in The Hammer. My personal favorite is O Sole Meato, the butcher shop.

A bell rang when I opened the door. I entered and was hit in the face by white. I squinted my eyes. Gad, it was bright. The whole place was shades of white and cream. Maybe that's why I always felt uncomfortable there. It was too clean.

Gertie, the middle-aged receptionist, poked her head out from behind a silky curtain divider.

"Hi, Gina. Mandy's just finishing up with a customer. Why don't you have a seat for a few minutes."

I smiled my thanks and plunked down on a white leather chair that looked brand new.

"Can I bring you a coffee?"

"Sure," I said. "Thanks." I never turned down caffeine.

The aspirin was starting to work. More coffee would do the trick. I had a little time, so I sat back to think. Something had been niggling at me about Wally. It was almost there—I just needed to concentrate. All that talk last night of jewelry and condos in Arizona. Things were clicking into place now. A pair of sapphire earrings. Paid for with cash. By a *doctor's* wife. That was key.

I had it! It all made sense. I was Nancy friggin' Drew after all. Nico would be wowed when I told him the goods.

Still had time to kill. I picked up the magazine that was on top of the pile. Had to smile at the name on the cover. *Association of Retired Seniors...*ARS for short.

I paged through it. The usual articles about older people who were famous actors and television personalities. An ad showing good-looking older people having the time of their lives aboard those long river-cruise ships. Several more ads for home-comfort products and face creams. I always find the ads in magazines just as entertaining as the articles.

One ad in particular caught my interest. This was because someone had taken a black felt pen and circled it. It read:

FLY BY NIGHT FUNERALS
Need Help? Short on cash?
From Rigor to Removal,
we do the whole thing.
Discreet Burials
Plenty of satisfied customers.
Call 555-PLANTUM
(555-752-6886)

I felt the blood leave my face. I recognized that phone number. It was the number I had used that morning to reach Jimmy.

Crap!

I quickly speed-dialed Sammy. It immediately went to voice mail.

I said a very bad word.

"Sammy, call me back *as soon as you can*," I hissed into the phone.

I sat for a moment listening to my heart pound. But I'm really not good at sitting and doing nothing. So I phoned the number in the ad. Again, it went to voice mail. A shaky voice addressed me.

"You have reached Fly By Night Funerals... You plug 'em, we plant 'em. Please leave a number, and we will return your call as soon as possible."

The machine beeped at me. I clicked off without leaving a message.

I stared at the phone in my hand. Almost immediately it began to sing "Shut Up and Drive."

"What's up?" said Sammy.

"Fly by Night Funerals. Spill it," I said, keeping my voice low.

"Ah."

Long pregnant pause.

"Maybe we can do an information trade," I said. "How much do you want to know about what went down the other night at La Paloma?"

"With Wally the Wanker? I want to know. But I don't want the cops to know," said Sammy.

"So we keep it to ourselves," I said. "And Nico. Gotcha."

"Maybe we should meet in person. La Paloma at four?"

It was just after three now. "I'll be there," I said.

I bolted up from the leather chair and made for the door.

"Hey! Gina, where are you going?"

I looked back over my shoulder. Mandy stared at me. She had a white coffee mug in her hand.

"Gotta meet Sammy! It's urgent."

She nodded and waved her free hand at me. Being part of the family, she understood.

TEN

I picked Nico up and we got to La Paloma at five to four. I said hi to Giacomo and Guido, who worked the kitchen, and then we went to hug Vera. She was a comfortable, soft-all-over bundle.

Sammy came in the back way. He usually came in through the back alley if he could. "Get in the habit of doing the smart thing, so it becomes a habit" is rule thirty-one in *Burglary for Dummies*.

"*Ciao bella*." He gave Vera a kiss on both cheeks. Then he turned and did the same to me.

"Espresso, Sammy?" Vera was already moving to the machine.

"Not this time. But I could do with a plate of your cannoli, bella."

Yum. I go all limp for cannoli.

"Your car is out back, Gina," said Sammy. "I had someone drop it off."

"Great! Thanks." I dragged him by the arm into the dining room and shoved him into a chair. Nico carried the plate of cannoli and sat beside him.

"First things first." I plunked down in the chair opposite him. "The body."

"Oh, that," said Sammy, leaning back. "Yeah, I figured there was a mix-up. Your box was supposed to go to the retirement home."

"The *retirement* home? Like they need more dead bodies? They don't create enough of their own?" This was just loony.

"Easy, sugar. It's simply a small business we're supporting. Jimmy is the manager."

I got this cold feeling.

"The manager of *what* small business?" said Nico. He reached for a cannoli.

"A funeral business. Nothing to get excited about. They just run it from the retirement home so there aren't that many questions."

Questions? I had a few questions. But before I could ask them, Sammy said, "Nobody notices a few extra bodies leaving a retirement home. Get it?"

I was starting to get it. I remembered the ad. *From rigor to removal,* it had said.

And then the answering machine message. *You plug 'em—we plant 'em.*

"They're running a business burying people who get offed?" I hissed as I was saying it.

"Eep!" Nico squeaked.

"We don't off them ourselves, sweetheart," said Sammy. "That's the joy of it. We just do the cleanup. We're actually providing a much-needed service. Or, at least, they are. I'm only a consultant."

"Jimmy? And Magda? And my great-aunt Rita?" I couldn't believe it. Those sweet, elderly folk? Okay, maybe they had checkered pasts, but...

Sammy went on. "The key to good business management is to provide a service that's got a demand for it. Jimmy nailed it. People are distressed when they have a body hanging around. They pay well. So the Last Chance Club...they got more business than they can handle."

"Isn't this sort of illegal?" Nico said. He was twisting a linen napkin in his hands.

"Embalming and burying isn't illegal. And Freddie is a licensed funeral worker guy, although I don't know that he's kept up his license. Tends to forget things, what with the dementia."

Dementia?

"Once he forgot to dress a guy after the embalming. You wouldn't believe what a little extra fluid can do to some parts. We don't do open casket anymore."

Nico yelped.

I tried not to visualize it. I really did.

"Look, I know you got a thing about certain aspects of the family business," Sammy said to me. "We got nothing to do with the plugging end of it, doll. I promise."

My mind was like a whirligig. Whatever the hell that was.

"But why? Why would they do this?"

Sammy's voice perked up. "Oh. Well, that's easy. The Last Chance Club. They want to go on a bus trip to Vegas. You know. Hit the tables, see the shows. It costs big bucks to rent a bus to go that distance. Not to mention hotel rooms, and all those buffets. And they need supervision."

No argument there.

"I like Vegas," said Nico, all eager. "I could supervise."

I groaned. "You'll be doing it on your own then, Nico." No way was I playing den mother to a bunch of randy pensioners in Sin City.

Then something else hit me.

"So *that's* what the coffins are for!" I said. "The ones in the chicken coop."

Sammy hesitated. I could guess why. I watched his gnarly face. Then something clicked in, and he smiled.

"You got it. They don't got a lot of space in the retirement home. So we're helping them out by storing them at the coop. It's only for a little while. Got a big shipment coming in soon."

Shipment?

"So they'll get used up," Sammy finished.

Shipment of bodies?

"I really don't want to know about this," I said, hitting my hand against my head.

"'Course you don't, doll. You got a lot on your mind, with the wedding and all. Which reminds me. What's the scoop on Wally the Wanker?"

"Hold on a sec. One thing first." It was my turn to smile like the Cheshire cat. "The coffins. They're from Canton, right?"

Sammy squirmed. "You figured that out?"

I nodded. "Great way to smuggle counterfeit money into the country."

Now he cursed. "You always were the smart one. Sure you don't want to join the business? I could use you."

"Not a chance," I said. But I was secretly pleased. "Is it in the satin lining, or is there a false bottom?"

"False bottom," Sammy said.

"What are you talking about?" said Nico.

I turned to him. "Remember the counterfeit five-dollar bills Carmine got caught passing a few weeks ago?"

One hand shot to his mouth. "Are we doing...?"

"I'm not doing anything, Nico. Neither are you. And hopefully neither is Sammy anymore." I gave him the evil eye.

Sammy nodded his head in agreement. "That was a bad idea. Lousy quality. Paulo was right. It's careless not to oversee your own operations."

That was another place I didn't want to go.

"Let's move on. Aunt Vera? " I yelled to the back. She came to the swinging door, wiping her hands on a tea towel.

"Yeah?"

"Come here for a sec. Bring Uncle Vito. You'll want to hear this. It's about Wally."

ELEVEN

Vera and Vito came out to the public area and joined us at the table for six. They sat down. I stood up. I think better on my feet.

"You gonna tell us what happened with that Wally, Gina? 'Cause I don't get it. Why dump a body here? It's a nice place." Vera fiddled with the apron spread across her ample lap.

I turned to Sammy. "We're keeping this between us, right? Not telling the cops unless we have to? 'Cause I can't prove it, you know. It's just conjecture."

Sammy nodded. "You go, girl."

I smiled and leaned forward, putting both hands on the white tablecloth. "Wally the Wanker was making a little extra on the side, peddling OxyContin to the upper classes. Nice work, if you can get it. But then his source started to shut down. Wanted out of it. So Wally resorted to his high-school trade. Remember what that was, Nico?"

Nico shivered. "Blackmail."

All eyes swung to Nico.

"Sonamabeech." You could see Aunt Vera calculating what Nico had been in the frame for back then.

"Got it in one," I said, straightening up. I talk with my hands a bit, so they need to be free.

"So. Wally started to blackmail his source because he wouldn't come through with the dope anymore. And the source didn't think that was nice. So he took out Wally with a .38." I flicked my arm to the side. "Doesn't matter where. Then he dumped the body on the back steps of La Paloma, that noted 'family' hangout, when no one was looking."

"I don't get it," said Vera.

"The killer hoped the take-out would be put down to us," Sammy said. His brown eyes were piercing.

I nodded.

"Well, that won't happen. We've taken care of it. No body, no crime. Nothing to report." Sammy sat back and folded his spindly arms. "I'll spread a rumor that Wally left The Hammer for his health. So all that remains is you naming the killer, sugar."

This was the fun part. I grinned and pointed to the ring on my left hand.

"You know me. I notice jewelry—can't help it. And that sapphire ring was niggling at me." I paused for effect. "Doctors make a lot of money, but they don't make *that* much. That night in this restaurant, Mrs. Drake was wearing the ring she bought from my store last month. You wanna talk money—that rock makes my twenty-four-grand engagement ring look like a dollar-store bauble. Then this week she shows up at Ricci Jewelers, wanting a pair of matching earrings. The thing about earrings…they come in twos. Double the rocks, so double the price. And she wants to pay cash."

I looked at Sammy. The map lines on his face signaled that his brain was in full processing mode.

"Doctors don't get paid in cash," Sammy said.

I continued. "At the shower, Pinky told us that Sherry Drake and her hubby had just purchased a condo in Scottsdale, Arizona. Lots of money being thrown around quite suddenly. Then I remembered that she—Mrs. Drake—entered the restaurant alone the night Wally was killed. Dr. Drake came in about ten minutes later. That's because he was dumping the body out back. Then he drove around the front, parked and pretended to just get here."

"But—" started Aunt Vera.

"Wait, Vera. Gina will explain," said Uncle Vito patiently. His chubby hands rested on his ample belly.

"What better way to score illicit Oxy than from a bona fide doctor," Sammy said. "Then the doc refuses to play anymore, and Wally tries to blackmail him. Ah, Wally. You stupid bastard."

"He was *a blackmailer*, Sammy." Nico had his chin up and his arms crossed. "I know Wally's dead now, but I can't feel sorry for him. Even if he was in the family."

"That's why we're not going to say a word about it," I said, pulling out a chair.

"No body, no crime. You see a body around here?" Sammy waved both his arms.

Aunt Vera looked around the room. "What body? We got another body?"

Uncle Vito sighed and shook his head.

Sammy kissed me, reached for a cannoli and left the restaurant. Vera and Vita went back to the kitchen. I stayed sitting with Nico to finish the last cannoli.

"So. Two down," I said, after swallowing the last yummy bite. "I solved the *Who Killed Wally* case. I figured out the *Counterfeit Coffin Caper*."

Nico smiled. "Well done, Nancy Drew."

I met his eyes. "We have one more thing to do."

"Tonight? Your car?"

"Yup. Pick you up at seven thirty. Wear black."

TWELVE

"Thanks for helping out, Pete. I didn't know who else to ask. The Last Chance Club people will be there. But they're just too old and frail to do any digging."

"I still don't understand how that box of Seb's got buried in the graveyard in the first place," said Pete.

"Sometimes the greatest mysteries of life are best left that way," said Nico from the backseat.

"Nico, that doesn't make any sense at all," said Pete.

"Then my job is done," Nico said with a smile.

It wasn't late at night. It wasn't even eight o'clock. But already the sky was pitch-black. The city lights blocked out most of the stars.

We were all wearing black, even Pete. I'd told him it was a requirement. Actually, it was. Chapter 12 of *Burglary for Dummies* states, "Always wear black for any kind of night job. It doesn't reflect light and also makes you look pounds slimmer."

This could be handy when your arrest photo is plastered all over the front page of the daily newspaper. Italians are a vain lot.

Of course, Pete and Nico wore black in different ways. Pete looked seriously bad-ass. Nico appeared as if he had walked off the cover of *GQ*.

I signaled left and turned my car into the Black Chapel Cemetery. Then I drove down a narrow lane and pulled up behind a white SUV.

"There they are!" I could see a bunch of short people gathered around an open grave. Mario, Jimmy, Mad Magda and a few other elderly folk were sitting on folding lawn chairs. I made out several more bodies—larger male ones—on the other side of the grave.

I got out of the car and started to pick my way through the gravestones. Pete and Nico followed.

"Oh Christ, Lou. It's the crazy broad." Bertoni's voice! I would know it anywhere.

Yup, there he was, the whole skinny, greasy package. He was standing beside the rest of the cousins from Buffalo. Lou, the quiet one. And Joey, who used to follow me around with a supersize crush. They were, of course, wearing black.

At least Joey I could tolerate. He was as big as a Brinks truck, with a surprising heart of gold.

"Hi, Joey," I said, waving a hand. "How's things?"

He walked over to us. The guy was massive, even taller than Pete.

"Hey, Gina," he said, nodding his round head. "Same ole, same ole. Good to see you, Pete." He held out a big hand, and Pete shook it.

"What are you doing here?"

"Helping the Last Chance Club. We're the muscle. What about you?"

"Hey! He's got a shovel." Bertoni pointed at Pete. "Are they horning in on our business, Joey?"

Damn that Bertoni!

"We're not doing anything!" I yelled back. "I'm here to get my box. It got buried last night."

Joey looked at me oddly. "You bury boxes in the graveyard."

"Not usually," I said. "This was a... special occasion." Okay, so that sounded ridiculous. "And actually, I didn't bury it. I think you guys did."

"Wait a minute," said Bertoni. "We planted a coffin last night. Why are you digging up a body?"

"It isn't a body! That was all a mistake. Mario got it wrong. You took the wrong box from my store."

"So what's in the box then, if not a body?" said Joey.

"Never mind," I said primly. "It's not your box."

"Hey, fat bum, give. What's in the box?" said Bertoni.

"Who are you calling 'fat bum'?" Now I was mad. "You greasy piece of festering weasel. I'll 'fat bum' your face with a two-by-four!" Both of my hands went into fists, and I stomped forward.

"Hey, Gina." A big hand landed on my shoulder. It was Joey's. "Cool it. Ignore Bertoni. He doesn't know what he's talking about. I always loved your fat bum."

Pete guffawed.

I got angrier. I wrestled out of Joey's hold.

"It's not—oh for crissake." My hand slapped my forehead. "I don't have to explain my butt to you guys. *Jeez*, why do I have you morons for relatives?"

I flung my arms around like a windmill. "All I want is to live a normal life. Run my shop. Get married. Go on a little honeymoon. Have a few dozen kids. Is that too much to ask? And then you losers have to go and take away the *wrong* box—"

"What box?"

We all turned. The voice came from several feet behind us, and I'd heard it recently.

Cripes! The cops.

"Well, well, well. If it isn't Gina Gallo. The girl with the longest confession."

"That's getting old, Spense." I rolled my eyes. "What did you do, follow us here?"

Pause. "Yeah, yeah. Like I don't have enough to do."

"You *did* follow us. Have you got a tail on me?" Now that pissed me off.

Bertoni hooted. "Has she got a tail on her! Oh yeah."

"Shut UP!" I yelled like a harpy.

"Stay away from her, Spense," Pete growled. He stepped in front of me. Nice thought, but it meant I had to move around him like we were dancing in order to see.

"And Malone from the *Star*. Big surprise. So what brings you to Black Chapel Cemetery in the middle of the night? I can't wait. This is gonna be good."

"It's not the middle of the night, and we're not robbing graves," I explained patiently.

"We're digging up treasure," Nico said.

115

If looks could kill, mine would have struck Nico dead on the spot.

I didn't know the tall cop standing next to Spense. He looked baffled.

"Digging up treasure. " Spense tsk-tsked. "Grave robbing. You've really come down in the world, Gina. And trespassing to boot."

"Not trespassing." I thought quickly. "We own this."

"What? The *cemetery*?"

"Not the whole thing." I swallowed hard. "But this section of it is all Gallo. Gallo plots."

"Just waiting for us all to die," said Nico.

I nodded vigorously.

Spense didn't look convinced.

"So you're digging up treasure on your own gravesite. Mind explaining how it got there in the first place?"

"He buried it." Three voices rang out. Nico pointed at Joey. Joey pointed at Bertoni. Bertoni pointed at Mario.

"And why did you bury treasure in a graveyard?"

"We thought it was a body," Bertoni said.

"Oops," muttered Nico.

"Whose body?" barked Spense.

"Mine," Jimmy piped up. He had wandered over from the other side of the hole.

"But you're not dead yet," said Spense. There was an unnaturally high pitch to his voice. I was starting to feel sorry for him.

"We misplaced it," said Jimmy, all grumbly like. "I'm always losing things."

"You misplaced your body."

Pete chortled then. Really, I was wondering how he had managed to hold off for so long.

"Yeah. And then we found it again," said Jimmy. "It's over here." He signaled with a skinny arm.

We all traipsed over to the open grave. Mad Magda, Great-Aunt Rita, Mrs. Pesce and another old guy sat on their walker chairs on the other side of the hole, waiting. One of them gestured into the hole.

"Poor Dino," Mad Magda crooned. "So sad to go that way."

"What way?" said Spense.

Crap. None of us knew. There was an awkward silence.

"You know. Like, he didn't recover," Nico said helpfully. "He died from it."

"And now he's dead," said Bertoni, nodding his greasy head.

Pete made a sound like a donkey.

"I heard he died of heart failure," said Rita.

"Two slugs from a .38 will do that," whispered Joey.

Nico squeaked beside me.

"Don't he look natural," said Mrs. Pesce hastily.

"He don't look natural at all," my great-aunt snapped. "You can't even see him. He's in a pine box."

"Chinese pine," Nico added. "Imported from China. We even have the bill."

"Pine is natural. I still say he looks natural," said Mrs. Pesce. She turned her pug face to Rita in a challenge.

More donkey sounds.

"So you see, sergeant, I really don't think there's anything to charge us with here," I said. "We're merely saying our farewells to a deceased resident of the Holy Cannoli Retirement Home."

"On account of he died recently," said Jimmy.

"And retrieving a box that got buried by mistake," I finished.

"There's no body in it. You can look," Nico said generously.

Spense stared at each of us, one after the other. Mrs. Pesce grinned and waved at him.

"So if this here's a burial, where's the priest?" asked the tall cop.

Crap. I forgot about him. Silence again. I held my breath. Then...

"It's one of those no-name funerals. Do-it-yourself," said Jimmy.

"In the dark." Spense frowned.

"After-hours. Makes it cheaper," piped up Mags.

All present members of the Last Chance Club nodded.

"Dino would have wanted it this way. He was always a cheap bastard," said Mrs. Pesce.

The donkey braying got louder.

Pete was bent over now. His back was shaking like he was about to expire. I hoped we wouldn't have another body on our hands.

"Freakin' loonies. No way am I writing this one up," said the tall cop. "You want to write this up?"

Spense growled.

"Let's get a coffee." The tall cop turned away.

"You people are all nuts," said Spense. "Every last one of you."

"You might want to leave now," said Nico under his breath. "It seems to be contagious."

THIRTEEN

We watched the two cops amble out of sight. I gave a sigh of relief and then turned to Mario.

"Okay, so we better get going, digging this thing up. Where's the box, Mario?"

Mario's cherub face twisted. "What box?"

I sighed. "The box you took from my jewelry store. You know. The one Bertoni and gang buried last night." Jeesh. Did I have to explain everything?

Still no clue on Mario's face.

"The wrong box was delivered to Nico's place next door." I tried to be patient. "It was supposed to be a statue."

"What was it instead?" Pete's voice came from behind me.

Uh-oh. We all turned to face Pete. He didn't know about this part.

I decided to keep it that way.

"And when you guys came back to pick it up, you went to my place instead," I explained to Mario. "And took the box that was in my office. By mistake."

Mario still looked blank.

I continued, getting more and more exasperated. "Mario, you are such a screw-up. How can you not remember? Carved walnut chest, about four feet by two feet. Ring a bell?"

Jeesh, this was tedious.

Two lights came on in Mario's eyes. "Oh, *that* box. I thought it was Little Louie."

I paused a beat.

"Little—who?"

"Little Louie."

Jimmy snorted. "Little Louie ain't little. He's at least three hundred pounds."

"That's a nickname," said Mad Magda. "On account of he's the younger Louie in the family. Not our family," she added hastily.

"Louie wouldn't fit in a four-foot box. He'd need a supersize," said Jimmy.

"So you thought it was Little Louie," I said, losing patience. "Well, it wasn't. My inheritance is in that box. Hundreds of thousands of dollars in bonds and stocks and cash, from Seb's studio."

"The cash is probably phony," Magda whispered to Jimmy.

I gave them a dirty look.

"So you can see why I'm kind of anxious to get it back. Sammy said you buried it last night. So is it here?"

Mario gulped. "Sort of."

This was getting squirrely.

"So where is it? We have to start digging and get out of here before the cops come back."

Another pause. Mario started fiddling with his hands.

"Um...the thing is...I followed the instructions left for Little Louie."

Pregnant silence.

"Uh-oh," said Nico. I glanced at him. He looked miserable.

"What instructions?"

Mario squirmed. "They wanted him cremated."

"I knew it," murmured Nico.

"YOU BURNED MY BOX?"

Joey started to howl.

"Do you want the ashes?" said Mario helpfully. "They're in a nice vase. We could reuse the vase."

"Get out of my way! I'm gonna kill him."

Mario backed away. "Gina, take it easy. I didn't know."

"Gimme that shovel." I grabbed it from Pete.

Mario put up his hand like a stop sign. "No, Gina, you don't want—HELP!"

I swung the shovel like a baseball bat.

"Yikes!" yelled Mario, stepping back out of reach. "Somebody stop her!"

I swung it again, and Pete caught my arm. Mario leaped farther back and disappeared from sight.

"Shit!" he yelled.

I wrenched away from Pete and threw the shovel to the ground. Then I raced to the edge of the open grave, along with everyone else.

"Don't think hiding down there is going to save you!" I yelled over the moans coming from the bottom.

I was gonna kill him. He was already in a grave, and I was gonna kill him so he could stay there forever.

I made to leap into the hole and was caught by one arm.

"Don't be foolish, Gina," said Pete, hauling me back from the edge. "That's a long way down."

I shook off his grip. Then I leaned over and filled both of my hands with dirt.

"Son of a bitch!" I yelled. I pitched the dirt at Mario, who was writhing and moaning. Then I reached down for more dirt and pitched that.

Bertoni was snickering like a hyena. Joey was roaring with laughter.

"Help the poor doofus up, Joey," said Magda. "He may have broken something."

"You nincompoop! You useless wad of... of..."

"Toilet paper? Chewing gum?" Nico offered helpfully.

I was shoveling dirt onto Mario with my right foot now. Pete dragged me back from the edge again.

"He cremated my inheritance!" I wailed as Pete swung me around. "At least a million dollars!" I started to cry real tears.

Pete chuckled and reached for me. "Aw… sweet thing. Don't cry. It doesn't matter. You don't need it. I have tons of money."

Everyone went quiet.

I stiffened. I pushed back from his arms and frowned at him. "What do you mean?"

Pete shrugged and crossed his big arms over his chest. "At least ten million. I inherited from my grandfather. He invented a heart-stent thingy that all the hospitals use."

It took a moment for my brain to process the words. Then I gulped. "You have ten million dollars?"

"Actually, *we* do. I changed my will last week." He sounded smug.

The chatter started back up. I took a deep breath. "We have ten million dollars that I DIDN'T KNOW ABOUT?"

Pete backed away from me. "Okay, probably I should have told you before now. But I didn't want you marrying me for my money."

The silence, as they say, was deafening.

"Uh-oh." Nico winced. "Probably you shouldn't have said that last bit." He backed up.

"YOU THOUGHT I WOULD MARRY YOU FOR YOUR—" I choked on that last word. Then I swung around. "Where's that shovel?"

"Pete, I think you better…" Nico signaled with a hand.

Pete took off at a run. "Mario, wait up!"

"I'm gonna kill him," I said, grabbing the shovel with both hands.

"Probably you should wait until after the wedding and then kill him," said Jimmy.

Magda nodded. "It's tradition."

ACKNOWLEDGMENTS

I am fortunate to have friends in the crime-writing world, who are generous with support and encouragement. Cathy Astolfo, Alison Bruce, Cheryl Freedman and Joan O'Callaghan—thank you for reading my early versions and laughing in all the right places.

Don Graves—thank you for appreciating and celebrating the wacky side of crime humor. Your reviews have made a big difference to me.

Bob Tyrrell at Orca Books—thank you for taking a chance on an unconventional comedy writer five years ago.

Ruth Linka—thanks, once again, for making it all come together in this book. You and your team make every step of the publishing journey a pleasure.

Library Digest compared **MELODIE CAMPBELL** to Janet Evanovich. But comedy and mystery writing came to Melodie after she was a bank manager, marketing director and college instructor. Melodie has over two hundred publications, including one hundred comedy credits and forty short stories, and has won ten awards for short fiction. In 2014 Melodie won both the Derringer Award and the Arthur Ellis Award for *The Goddaughter's Revenge*. She is the executive director of Crime Writers of Canada and lives outside of Toronto, Ontario.

DON'T MISS
Gina Gallo's
OTHER ADVENTURES!

"Campbell tells a hilarious story of the
goddaughter of a mafia leader drafted into
a jewel-smuggling operation."
— *Ellery Queen Mystery Magazine*

"Campbell's comic caper is just right for Janet
Evanovich fans. Wacky family connections and
snappy dialog make it impossible not to laugh."
— *Library Journal*

RAPID READS
WWW.RAPID-READS.COM

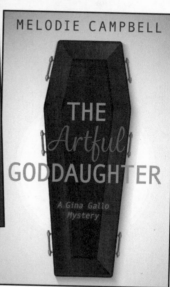

2014 Arthur Ellis Award
winner for Best Novella
2014 Derringer Award
winner

MELODIE CAMPBELL

THE
GODDAUGHTER'S
REVENGE

MELODIE CAMPBELL

THE
Artful
GODDAUGHTER

*A Gina Gallo
Mystery*

"A novella with legs and laughter…Strong plot, great zingers and imagery that draws you in and just doesn't let go…The scam is delightful, the plot, setting and dialogue move with page turning intensity which makes the Artful Author's third crime ride a blast and a laugh."

— Don Graves

RAPID READS
WWW.RAPID-READS.COM